I'll Play With You

by **Mary McKenna Siddals**
illustrated by **David Wisniewski**

Clarion Books • New York

Clarion Books
a Houghton Mifflin Company imprint
215 Park Avenue South, New York, NY 10003
Text copyright © 2000 by Mary McKenna Siddals
Illustrations copyright © 2000 by David Wisniewski

Type is 22-point Esprit.
Illustrations executed in watercolor and Color-Aid cut papers.

Printed in Hong Kong.

Library of Congress Cataloging-in-Publication Data
Siddals, Mary McKenna.
I'll play with you / by Mary McKenna Siddals ; illustrated by David Wisniewski.
p.   cm.
Summary: A child speaks to the sun, wind, clouds, rain, stars, and moon, asking to play with them.
ISBN 0-395-90373-4
[1. Play—Fiction.] I. Wisniewski, David, ill. II. Title.
PZ7.S5653 2000
[E]—dc21   99-057849

SCP 10 9 8 7 6 5 4 3 2 1

With thanks to my mother,
Dorothea McKenna,
whose love of nature
has enriched my life
and inspired my writing
                    —M. M. S.

For the Sneddon family
                    —D. W.

I'll play with you, Sun.
Meet me outside.

I'll help you make shadows.
I'll hide while you climb.

Then poke through the branches
and tickle me warm.

I'll play with you, Wind.
Just give a whistle.

I'll come running,
and you whoosh right through me.

Then swirl up the dust
and make the leaves dance.

I'll play with you, Clouds.
Pile up in the sky.

You make some pictures.
I'll guess what they are.

Then puff up and stretch out,
and I'll guess again.

I'll play with you, Rain.
Don't grumble at me!

Just fill up the puddles
so I can go splashing,

and when you're all finished,
make me a rainbow.

I'll play with you, Stars.
Peep out from the dark.

You twinkle,
and I'll try to count you.

Then I'll make a wish,
and you make it come true.

I'll play with you, Moon.
Just come to my window.

I'll open my curtains
and let you shine in.

You be my night-light,

and I'll have sweet dreams.